FRANKENSTEIN

FRANKENSTEIN

By Mary Wollstonecraft Shelley

Adapted by Diana Stewart
Illustrated by Gary Kelley

Raintree Publishers · Milwaukee · Toronto · Melbourne · London

Library of Congress Number: 81-5216

2 3 4 5 6 7 8 9 0 85 84 83

Printed in the United States of America.

Library of Congress Cataloging in Publication Data

Stewart, Diana.
  Frankenstein.

  (Raintree short classics)
  Summary: The monster was supposed to be man's
benefactor, but, scorned for his ugliness, he swears
revenge on his creator and the human race.
  [1. Monsters — Fiction. 2. Horror stories]
I. Kelley, Gary. II. Shelley, Mary Wollstonecraft,
1797-1851. Frankenstein. III. Title. IV. Series.
PZ7.S84878Fr   [Fic]   81-5216
ISBN 0-8172-1674-X   AACR2

CONTENTS

PROLOGUE

A letter to Mrs. Saville in England, written by Robert Walton, from somewhere in the Arctic Ocean, August 19, 17—.

My dear sister,

I write first to assure you I am still alive and well. But second, I want to tell you a strange story.

Our ship is surrounded by ice. Now and then the seas churn, the huge chunks of ice break up, and we are able to move on ahead. The other day I stood looking out over the great frozen wilderness. To my amazement, across the ice I saw a dog sled. As it drew near, I made out the form of a man — a giant. He was gone before I could see more than that.

The next day, the ice broke again and we moved forward. It was then that we came upon a second sled floating on a huge raft of ice. The man beside it was nearly frozen. Quickly we took him on board and carried him to my cabin. He was more dead than alive, but after several hours he began to recover somewhat. For days I have looked after him. He is still very ill, and I fear for his life.

He said nothing for several days, but now he is more open with me. We have become friends. His name is Victor Frankenstein. I am very fond of him. He is intelligent, well-educated, kind and gentle. Something, however, is troubling him greatly.

Last night Victor said he had a story to tell me. I shall record his tale in this letter to you. Oh, I feel such pity for my new friend. He has obviously suffered so much. His story must be terrible indeed.

FRANKENSTEIN BEGINS HIS TALE TO ROBERT

I was born in Geneva, Switzerland, my dear Robert. My family has always been honorable and well-respected. My parents were kind and loving, and I had the happiest of childhoods. Until I was five years old, I was an only child. At that time, my parents adopted an orphan girl — Elizabeth — whose father, an Italian nobleman, had been killed.

Elizabeth was just a year younger than me and beautiful in both body and spirit. Her hair was of the brightest gold. Her eyes were a cloudless blue. Her lips, her brow, her whole face held a look of such sweetness. I loved her from the first moment I set eyes on her.

We were brought up together and called each other cousins. Later, my parents had two other children, William and Ernest, and we were a very happy family.

I was blessed also with a dear friend — Henry Clerval, son of a Geneva merchant. Henry loved tales of adventure and romance. He wrote songs and stories of heroes and the Knights of the Round Table. I myself was not interested in these stories of make-believe; nor was I interested in languages, history or politics. What interested me was natural science, and I read all the books I could find. I wanted to learn all there was to learn about the body, mind, and spirit of Man — the secrets of heaven and earth. I could not know that these studies set my fate. My work was to bring me complete and terrible destruction.

When I reached the age of seventeen, my parents decided to send me to a university in Germany to complete my education. But before the date was set for me to leave, a disaster occurred in my family.

My dear mother was taken ill. Not all my medical knowledge could save her. On her deathbed she called Elizabeth and myself to her. She joined our hands together and said:

"My children, my dearest wish is that one day you two may marry. I know that this will bring all your future happiness. Elizabeth, take my place in the family. Be a mother to my young children. Be a joy to your adopted father. I go cheerfully to my death with the hope of meeting you in another world."

My most beloved mother was dead, but the living had to go on. Elizabeth hid her sorrow and worked to carry out my mother's last wishes. She devoted herself to the children and my father. She was the sunshine in a dark and gloomy home.

At last the time came for me to leave my family, my beloved Elizabeth, and my dear friend Henry. There in Germany I began a whole new life. My professors opened new worlds for me. I studied all the natural sciences. I read of men who had explored the workings of the earth below and the nature of the heavens above. The more I learned the more I became filled with the desire to go beyond what other scientists had done. I would be a pioneer. I would explore unknown powers and show the world the deepest mysteries of creation.

For two years I worked long and hard. I read, did experiments, and attended lectures. My professors were delighted with my progress. I pushed farther and farther into the unknown. I asked myself: Where does life come from?

I studied the physical body. I learned everything there was to learn about anatomy — bones, blood, organs, the brain. Nights I spent in the graveyard examining the corpses there. I sneaked into the charnel-house — the house where those who had recently died were placed. I saw how death took the bloom of life from a cheek. I

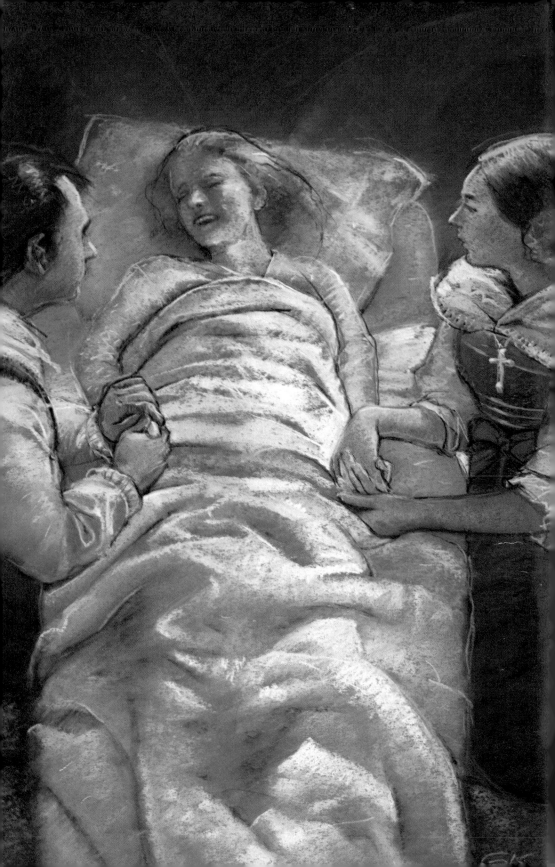

watched the worms take over the eye and brain of the dead. I noted what happened to the human organs when life seeps out of the body.

After weeks and months of study, I made my great discovery. What I am about to tell you is true! I discovered the secret of life and death! More than that, I knew that I was capable of giving life and movement to dead matter! I became consumed with the desire to carry out an experiment. I wanted nothing more than to put my knowledge to use.

I see by the look in your eye, Robert, that you want to know my secret. But listen! Learn from my experience! This knowledge has brought me nothing but the darkest, blackest misery and pain.

I had such confidence in my power that I was determined to begin with the highest form of life — Man. I would create a man and give him life. But I didn't want my creation to be an ordinary man. He would be the most wonderful human being ever created.

First, I built a laboratory in the attic of my house. Then from the graves and charnel-house I gathered the pieces. I made my creature eight feet in height, and each part of him was large to fit his height. For weeks I worked on him. My cheeks become pale and thin. My eyes were red and strained from working in the dim light of the attic.

Night after night I returned to the charnel-house and then the butcher shops to gather more bones and pieces of flesh. The summer months passed. Finally one cold and dreary night in November, my creature was completed!

The hour was one in the morning when I looked at my creation. It was still just dead flesh and bones, but I knew that in one short moment I would give it life. I gathered my chemicals around me and prepared to put the spark of life into the creature lying at my feet.

The moment of creation came! My superhuman man was alive! My creature was born!

My candle was only a glimmer of light, but in that glimmer I saw the dull yellow eye of the creature open. A hand

and arm jerked. I heard the first gasping breaths come from the cold and twisted mouth.

Oh, how can I describe my emotions when I first saw life in this terrible being I had created! How can I describe this terrible wretch I had formed? I had thought that each part of him I had gathered was beautiful, but now that life burned in the body, I saw I had created a monster! His hair was a shining black, long and flowing. His teeth were a pearly white. But these wonderful features only made his watery eyes look more terrible. His lips were straight and black. His yellow skin barely covered his muscles and veins.

For this terrible monster I had studied and worked so hard for nearly two years. For this I had worked months with little rest and food. For this I had ruined my health. The beauty of my dream disappeared the second my creature came to life. As I looked at this hideous monster, my heart was filled with horror and disgust. I could not even look at my creation without feeling sick. I rushed from the room and threw myself on my bed, but the horror would not go away.

I slept, but my dreams were nightmares. I thought I saw Elizabeth — beautiful, lovely Elizabeth. I ran to her and kissed her, but her lips were dead. I held the corpse of my mother in my arms. Worms crawled from the folds of the gown she wore.

In terror I awoke from my sleep. My face was covered with sweat. My teeth were chattering, and my whole body began to tremble. Then by the light of the moon, I saw my monster standing at the foot of my bed. His eyes — if they could be called eyes — were staring at me. His jaws opened and he muttered some horrible sounds. A grin wrinkled his cheeks. One hand stretched out towards me. With a cry, I ran down the stairs and out into the night to escape him. There I stayed — walking, waiting, listening. I lived in terror of seeing my monster. No mortal man could have dreamed of a man so hideous as the one I had created and given life. Oh, what had I done!

FRANKENSTEIN'S FEVERED BRAIN

My dear Robert, I do not have words to describe the horror I felt. I became very ill with a fever of the brain. I think I would have died if I had not been rescued by my dear friend Henry. In the two years I had been working to create my monster, I had only written to my family a few times. They became worried about me. Henry came to find me. He arrived that terrible morning and found me outside my house, sick with terror.

Quickly he carried me to my room. I was half fainting at the thought of finding my monster there. But he had gone! I laughed and cried with relief.

"For God's sake, what is the matter?" Henry cried. "How ill you are! What has happened?"

"Do not ask me," I pleaded. "Oh, save me, Henry! Save me!" And I fainted.

Poor Henry! What he must have thought and felt. I was ill for a long time. The fever burned in my brain. For months I lay on my bed turning, twisting, burning in pain. During all that time Henry was my only nurse. The form of my monster was constantly in my mind. I ranted and raved, but thankfully Henry did not understand what I was saying.

Very slowly I began to recover. I could at last look at the world around me with some pleasure. Spring had come. Once again I could feel joy at the sight of the new leaves and flowers.

"Dearest Henry," I said at last, "how can I thank you? How can I ever repay you for saving my life?"

"Your return to good health is payment enough, Victor. But there is something you can do. If you feel well enough, write to Elizabeth and your father. They have been so worried about you. Put their minds at rest."

I wrote and received many loving letters in return. Henry and I enjoyed an entire year together. We talked, read, and walked through the fields and woods. My spirits were high. I had no way of knowing that disaster was about to strike.

Early in May I received a letter from my father: "My dear Victor. Oh, how can I tell you how unhappy we are! There is no easy way to break the terrible news. Your brother is dead. That sweet child William — so gentle and kind and warmhearted — has been murdered!

"Last Thursday evening, Elizabeth, the boys and I went to the woods above the house. As night came on, William and Ernest could not be found. Soon, however, Ernest returned alone. William had run away to hide during their game, and Ernest could not find him. We searched all night by the light of torches. About five in the morning, I discovered my lovely boy. He was stretched on the grass dead. The bruises of his murderer's fingers were on his neck.

"Come home, dearest Victor. Elizabeth blames herself for not taking better care of him. She weeps continually. Only you can comfort her. Come, Victor! We who love you are so unhappy!"

Poor William! Poor beautiful child! To die so terribly! How could anyone take the life of such a wonderful child!

Henry helped me prepare for the journey home. He was staying on at the university, and I would miss him greatly. I made the trip to Geneva as quickly as possible, but as I reached the edge of the city, I stopped my carriage for a moment. I had not been home in many years. Here I had played as a child and been happy, but now some terrible fear gripped me. I felt a thousand nameless evils. My body began to tremble. As I stood looking up at the mountains I loved, I could not move. I was frozen with fear. I knew without a doubt that fate was going to make me the most miserable of men.

Before I went home, I knew that I must visit the place where William's body had been found. As I approached the woods, a storm began. Rain poured over me. Lightning and thunder split the sky. The heavens were dark.

"William, my dear angel!" I cried. As I said these words, through the gloom I saw a figure come from the trees. I stood frozen in terror. I could not be mistaken! A flash of lightning showed me the face and form of the man. It was huge, twisted and hideous. It was none other than the evil creature I had created — the monster I had given life. In horror I watched him turn and disappear up the mountainside.

In a flash I knew the truth. I knew as surely as though the monster had spoken: Here was the murderer of my dear brother! Nothing human could have murdered such a beautiful child. The murderer had to be a monster — my monster! Two years had passed since I created him. Was this his first crime? Had I turned loose on the world an evil wretch who delighted in killing?

No one could understand the horror I felt as I turned my footsteps towards my home and family. What could I say to them? I wanted to cry out to the world that my monster had murdered my brother. I wanted him hunted and destroyed, but I had to remain silent. My family knew I had been ill for many months with a brain fever. Who would believe that I had really created a living creature like the world had never seen before!

It was early morning before I entered my father's house. Only my brother Ernest was awake, and tears fell from his eyes as he saw me. "Oh, Victor," he cried. "I am so glad you are home! We have a new sadness. William's murderer has been found, but the news brings us no joy."

"The murderer has been found?" I cried. "But who was able to follow him across the mountains and catch him?"

"I don't know what you mean," replied Ernest. "The murderer is none other than our faithful servant Justine."

"Justine!" I cried. "That poor girl has been accused? But it is impossible!"

"That is what we felt. Father took her in when she was alone and penniless. He has treated her with love and kindness. Who would have believed that the sweet girl could be capable of such a crime?"

"Why is she blamed?" I asked.

"On the night of William's murder, she disappeared. She did not return until the next morning. Then in her pocket was found Mother's locket that William had been wearing when he was killed. She was immediately arrested. Today is her trial."

"You are all mistaken," I said. "I know that poor, good Justine is innocent!"

Just then my father entered the room. He tried to greet me cheerfully, but I saw all the pain and misery in his face.

"Father, there has been a terrible mistake!" I cried. "Justine is not the murderer."

"I sincerely hope you are right," said my father sadly. "But I fear for her life."

We were soon joined by Elizabeth. In spite of the sorrow on her face, she was as beautiful as ever, and I loved her even more. I did my best to comfort her, but she wept for poor, beautiful William. She wept for the good, kind Justine.

All we could hope for was that during the trial, something would save Justine. Our hopes, however, were in vain. The story Justine told was indeed hard to believe. She told the jury that she had been visiting a friend when she heard that William was missing. She loved the boy very much and had gone to help in the search. All night she had tramped through the woods hoping to find him. At dawn she had lain down in a barn to rest and had fallen asleep. When she awoke, she returned home and heard that William was dead. It was only then she had put her hand in her pocket and discovered the locket. She had no idea how it had come to be there.

No one believed her but me. I knew the truth — and I could not speak to save her.

The next morning Justine was put to death for the crime she did not commit. Her death was my fault as surely as though I had killed her myself. Both William and Justine were the victims of my evil science.

Once again the fever burned in my brain. Justine and William could rest in peace — but I had to live and suffer and die a thousand deaths as I thought of the monster I had created. I wept bitterly. Nothing could bring me happiness. Elizabeth watched me grow more pale and thin. Her love reached out to comfort me, but I could not be comforted. I lived in constant fear that the monster would return and commit new crimes.

After a time, I felt a terrible need to get away from every living soul. My hope was to find some measure of peace in the mountains. Perhaps alone I could clear my thoughts and ease the aching in my heart. With this in mind, I left my home to wander and climb the mountain I loved best.

Mont Blanc was rocky, bare, and covered with snow. Its glittering peak shone in the sunlight over the clouds. Few men ever climbed this terrible mountain. As I hiked, for the first time in many days, my heart felt something like joy.

I had been climbing for several hours when I saw the figure of a man in the distance. He moved towards me with superhuman speed. He bounded over the ice and rocks that had taken me so long to cross. As the shape of the man became clear, a mist came over my eyes and I felt faint. Oh, terrible, hateful sight! It was the monster I had created, and I trembled in rage and horror.

"Devil!" I cried. "Do you dare come near me? I hate you with every fiber of my body! I will kill you. I will stamp you out like an evil insect. I will have my revenge for those victims you have murdered!"

"I expected this," said the monster. "All men hate the ugly and miserable, and I am more horrible than any other living creature. How, then, must I be hated. Even you — my creator — hate and reject me. You purpose to kill me. How dare you play with life like this!"

"Monster! The tortures of hell are too good for you! I gave you life. Now I will take the life from you!"

In a black rage, I sprang at him. He easily escaped me and said: "Be still! Have I not suffered enough? Will you make my life even more miserable? Beware, my creator. Life is sacred and I will defend myself from death. Oh, Frankenstein! Hear me! I am your creature, and I will be good and kind to you if you will only help me! Once I was good. Misery and unkindness have made me evil. Make me happy, and I will be good again! If you do as I ask, I will leave you and the rest of the world at peace. If you refuse me, I will destroy you! I will kill until the ground is red with the blood of your family and friends!"

"Be gone!" I cried. "I will not listen to you!"

"What can I say, Frankenstein? If you, my creator, hate me, what hope can I have from others? The world makes me its enemy. It is in your power to save me, if you will. Listen to my story, I beg of you!"

"Oh, curse the day I made you! Curse these hands that formed you!"

"Then save yourself from that curse," the monster said. "My future and yours are in your hands."

For the first time I felt my duty towards this monster as his creator. I had to listen to him. I had to know what he wanted from me. Therefore, I followed him across the ice and rocks to a cave. There he lighted a fire to warm us. Then he began his tale.

THE MONSTER'S TALE

Frankenstein, what can I tell you of the first weeks and months of my life? Before I left your house, I put on clothes, but the weather was cold. I was a poor, helpless, miserable wretch. I knew nothing of the world I had entered. Everything was new and strange to me. In those first days I had to learn about so many things. I learned to tell day from night. I learned about trees and snow and fields and mountains and the sun and the moon. I learned about feelings — cold and hunger and tiredness.

One day I found a fire that some beggars had left. I found that fire could keep me warm. I found that berries on the bushes could stop my hunger. I found that sleep could rest my aching body.

For many days I wandered. Then I came to a village. I looked in the window of a cottage and smelled food. I was hungry and entered the house, but I had hardly placed my foot within the door before the children began to scream and one of the women fainted. The whole village came at the sound of the alarm. Some people ran when they saw me. Others attacked. They threw stones and hit me with clubs. I escaped once again to the open country.

After several days I found a low wooden shed at the back of a cottage near the woods. Here I crawled in to escape from the cold and snow. I heard people moving around outside, but I was well hidden. That night I gathered straw for a bed. A chimney made up the back wall of my shed and kept me warm.

As I lay there thinking about the cruel people I had met, I

noticed a little light coming into my shelter from cracks in the wood around the chimney. I found that through these cracks I could see into the cottage. Three people were inside the small, neat room. One was a girl — young and lovely. Another was a young man. The third person was an old man.

The old man sat in a chair playing a guitar. At first, of course, I did not know what it was that made the beautiful sounds. I learned many things in the days to come. As the man played, the girl smiled. I had never seen such a wonderful sight. That smile made me feel things I had never felt before — a strange pain and pleasure. I was learning, you see, about love.

All day and all evening I watched them as they worked in the house and came and went in the yard. Only the old man remained inside. I found out later that he was blind. They made sounds to each other that I couldn't understand. Later I found that this was a language and that these sounds had a meaning.

All that night I thought about these people. They looked so kind. I longed to join them, but I remembered how the people in the village had treated me. I did not dare show myself.

In the days that followed, I waited and watched. Each day the young man would go out in search of wood for the fire while the girl worked. She dug up roots in the frozen garden or worked in the house — cooking and cleaning. There was love in that little cottage, but I could tell that my people were not happy. I could not imagine why. They had fire and food. They had clothes and shelter. It was not long before I found that some of the reason for their unhappiness was because they had so little food. I had been stealing part of that food during the night, but now I was determined to live only on the berries, nuts and roots I could find at night.

I also found another way to help them. Each night I took the young man's tools and went into the woods to cut firewood. I remember the first time I did this. The next morning the girl and young man opened the door and found a great pile of wood on the outside. They were amazed. It was a miracle. I noticed with pleasure that the man stayed home that day and helped the girl. From then on I cut wood for them each night.

I soon learned something about their language. I learned "fire," "milk," "bread," and "wood." I learned also the names of my family. The old man had only one name — father. The girl was sister, daughter, or Agatha. The man was brother, son, or Felix. Some words I came to know but did not understand: "love," "good," "dearest," "unhappy."

This is the way I spent my winter. I came to love my family in the cottage. I was happy when they were happy and I cried when they cried.

As the weeks went by, I discovered the miracle of spring. Oh, happy, happy earth! The trees that had been bare and brown now were covered with green. The air was warm and sweet with the smell of flowers. Plants of all kinds began to spring up from the ground. Now I was warm, and there was plenty of food to be found in the woods.

As I became happier, I began to dream. I dreamed I went to the door of the cottage. At first my family would be frightened of me, but then they would see that I was gentle and didn't mean them any harm. They would take me into their home and learn to love me. I wanted my dreams to come true; however, I knew that first I had to learn their language.

One warm day brought great happiness to my family. A beautiful woman came on horseback. Felix saw her first. "My little Arabian!" he cried. He laughed and held her to his chest and kissed her. I tried to listen to find out who the woman was. Felix called her Safie, but though she spoke, her language was not the same one my family used.

That night Felix began to teach the woman his language. I listened very carefully. I can brag that in the days that followed, I learned more quickly than Safie. I also listened

when Felix taught her about letters and writing. This opened a whole new world for me. I learned that the language was written in books. I listened as Felix and Agatha read to their visitor. From these books I learned about history and geography, about kings and heroes, and about government and religion. I found that my mind was very quick.

Other lessons impressed me. I heard about the differences in the sexes. I heard about mothers and fathers and children. I heard about love and friends and families. While all I learned made me happy in some ways, it also made me very sad. I learned that I was not like any other human being that lived on the face of the earth. I was stronger and bigger. I could stand heat and cold better. But I was ugly and deformed — a blot upon the earth. I had no father or mother. I had had no childhood. I had no past before the day you created me as a grown man. What was I then?

As the days passed, I learned more also about the family in the cottage. They had once lived in Paris — a rich and honored family. It was there that Felix had met and loved the Arabian woman Safie. Political troubles, however, drove them away. They had to leave or be killed. Safie had been left behind with all their wealth. This was why they had been so unhappy.

One night in the woods while I was looking for food, I came upon a suitcase that had been lost. When I took it back to my shed, I found it held clothes and books. I dressed myself in the clothes, and every day I read more and more about the world I lived in. I learned that men could be very cruel. I came to love goodness and hate wickedness.

But I had also found another book that changed my life. When I took off the clothes I had taken from your house, I discovered a diary in the pocket of the jacket — your diary, Frankenstein. I am sure you will remember this book. In it you had written a day by day account of my creation. What I read sickened me. God created man as beautiful — in his own image. You had made me ugly, horrible, different from other men. And the more I learned about the world, the better I realized how terrible I was. I saw myself reflected in the water of the pool, and I understood why men hated me.

During all this time of learning, another year went by. I grew very lonely. I wanted the friendship of other human beings.

One day Agatha, Felix and Safie went for a walk and left the old man alone. He sat in his chair, quietly playing his guitar. My heart beat quickly. This was the hour of my trial. With great fear I went to the door of the cottage and knocked.

"Who is there?" asked the old man. "Come in."

"Pardon me," I said. "I am cold and tired. I would be grateful if you would let me sit a moment with you and rest."

"Of course," said the old man. "Sit by the fire. You are a stranger in this land, I think. You speak French."

"Yes," I replied. "I was educated by a French family. I am grateful to you for your kindness. People seem to be afraid of me. They do not know that I am a kind and gentle person. I would never hurt anyone. I seek only friendship."

"I believe you have a strange story to tell," the old man said. "Let me hear it, and perhaps I can help you."

"Oh, wonderful man! I thank you with all my heart. You give me hope. With your help, perhaps I can find my way to people's hearts."

At this moment, I heard footsteps outside. I hadn't a moment to lose. I threw myself at the man's feet and grabbed him around the legs. "Oh, help me!" I cried. "Save and protect me! You and your family are the friends I seek. Do not fail me!"

"Great God!" exclaimed the old man. "Who are you?"

The cottage door opened before I could reply. Felix, Safie and Agatha entered. How can I describe their horror when they saw me? Agatha fainted. Safie rushed out of the cottage. Felix ran forward and tore me away from his father. With superhuman strength he threw me to the ground and beat at me with a stick. I could have torn him limb from limb. I could have killed him — but I didn't. I was in agony. Their rejection made me sick at heart. All my hopes were gone. In pain I ran from the cottage and hid once more in my shed.

Cursed, cursed creator! Oh, how I hated you! I swore to seek revenge for the miserable life you had given me.

The next morning when I awoke, I found that my family had gone. They had taken everything with them, and I never saw Safie, Felix, the old man, or my beautiful Agatha again. I no longer had any reason to stay there, but where was I to go? Who could I turn to? That was when I decided to find you. I would demand justice from you. You had to pay for what you had done to me. In your diary you had mentioned Geneva as your home. There I would go.

For many days I wandered. I had learned enough of geography to know which direction to take. Weeks passed. I traveled at night and stayed away from the villages. I was hiding in the woods one day when I heard the sound of voices. A young girl came running along the path. Even as I watched, her foot slipped and she fell into a large stream. I rushed from my hiding-place and jumped into the water. The force of the stream was strong, but I struggled and managed to get her to shore. Suddenly I heard a man approach. He saw me and ran forward, tearing the girl from my arms. When I stood, the man aimed a gun at me and fired. He then picked up the child and ran into the woods.

This then was the reward for my kindness. I had saved the child, and for my pains, I lay miserable and bleeding on the ground. Every feeling of kindness left me. I gnashed my teeth in rage and pain. I vowed hatred on all mankind.

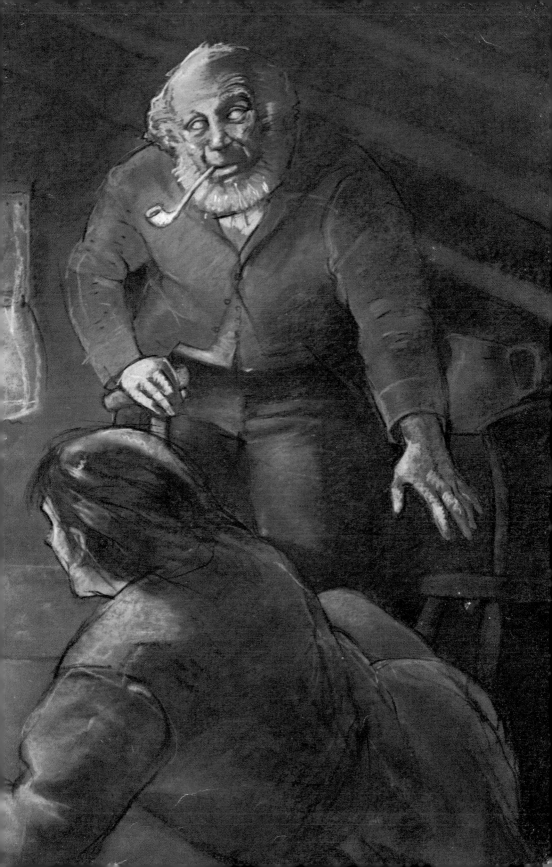

It took weeks for my wound to heal. Then, once more I continued my journey to Geneva. It was evening when I arrived on the edge of the city. I was tired and sick and hungry. As I stood there in the woods looking down on the town, a child ran towards me. I had a sudden thought. Here was a child — pure and beautiful. He was very young. Surely he had not lived long enough to be afraid of ugliness. I took hold of him as he passed me. "Child," I said, "listen to me. I won't hurt you!"

But he screamed and put his hands over his face. "Let me go!" he cried. "Monster! Ugly monster! Let me go! My name is Frankenstein! My father will kill you!"

"Frankenstein!" This boy belonged to my enemy. I had sworn revenge. This boy would be my first victim. He struggled and called me names. I grasped his throat to silence him, and in a moment he lay dead at my feet. I gazed on my victim. My heart was filled with joy. I hoped his death would bring you, my enemy, as much pain as you had given me.

As I looked at the child, I saw a locket around his neck. Inside was the picture of a beautiful woman. I remembered the face of my lovely Agatha. I remembered also how she looked when she saw me for the first time. Can you wonder that I felt such rage in my heart?

I left the spot where I had killed the child and came to a barn. A woman was sleeping on the straw. I had a plan. Someone else would suffer for the murder I had committed. She would pay for all the women who had looked on my face in horror. I placed the locket in the pocket of her jacket and fled.

I have waited here in the mountains above your home. I knew that I would find you here one day, and now I have. Now you must pay. I am alone and miserable. No living creature will have me. Here is what I ask of you, Victor Frankenstein. You must make another creature — a woman — as deformed and horrible as myself. I must have a companion like myself. This being you will create!

THE MONSTER'S REVENGE

Robert, (said Frankenstein) I felt sorry for the monster as he told his story. When he came to the murder of my beloved William, however, I burned with rage.

"I refuse," I said. "Shall I make another creature to run evilly through the world? Kill me, if you will. I will never do it!"

"You are wrong," the monster replied. "I am cruel because I am miserable. Make me happy and I will be kind and loving. Oh! My creator, let me be grateful to you for once. If you agree, neither you nor any other human being shall ever see us again. We will go to the wilds of South America. There my woman and I can live in peace and happiness."

I was moved by his words. "All right," I said. "I will make a companion for you. But you must give me your solemn oath that you will leave this country. You must promise to live in lands unknown to man."

"I swear," he cried, "by the sun, by the blue sky of heaven, and by the fire of love that burns in my heart. You will never see or hear of us again. Go home. Begin your work, I will be watching, and when you have finished, I will come to you."

He left me to make my way back down the mountain to my home. I wept bitterly as I went. My troubles were of my own making. Now I had to finish what I had thoughtlessly begun so long ago.

Weeks went by. I did not want to make the monster

angry, but I shrank in terror at the idea of creating another monster. Also, I had more to learn before I could create a female. I had heard of some discoveries made in England. I decided to leave Geneva and travel there. In England I could do my work away from the natural interest of my family.

On the day before I was to leave my home, my father called me to him. "My son," he said. "You know it was your mother's wish that you and Elizabeth should marry. I ask you now before you leave: Is it your wish to be married to her?"

"My dear father, I love Elizabeth tenderly and sincerely. I never saw any woman who I could love as I love her."

I was determined now to fulfill my promise to the monster as quickly as possible. Only when he was gone could I be free to marry my beloved Elizabeth and hope for happiness.

My father and Elizabeth were still worried about my health. Without my knowledge they arranged for Henry to leave school in Germany and travel with me to England.

It was good to see my friend again. Nearly a year had passed since I left him in Germany. What a difference there was between us now. I was weighted down with all my worries while he was alive with joy. Every new thing he saw delighted him. His soul was overflowing with love and friendship. I in turn loved him dearly and tried to hide my sorrow from him.

We had agreed to settle in London for a time. There was much to see, but for the most part, I let Henry go about the city alone. I had to study and collect the materials necessary for my new creation.

Several months passed. Then one day we received an invitation to visit friends in Scotland. This trip suited me well. I had everything I needed to begin my work. In Scotland I could find some deserted place to create my monster. So I gathered together my chemicals and other materials, and Henry and I set out for the north. Once we arrived, however, I left Henry with our friends to find a place to work.

"Enjoy yourself," I said to Henry. "I will leave you for a while. When I return, you will find me much happier."

Henry tried to persuade me to stay, but he saw that I wanted to be alone. "Go then, my dear friend," he replied. "Come back to me happy and healthy."

I found the ideal spot for my laboratory on an island off the coast of Scotland. The ground was rocky and barren. Only a few cows and five people lived there. On the whole island there were only three miserable huts. One of these I rented. Here I would make my creation.

Day and night I worked, but the labor was horrible to me. Often my heart was sick at the work of my hands.

One evening I sat in my laboratory. The sun had set. The sea pounded against the rocks. My new creature was nearly completed, and for the first time I allowed myself to think about what I was doing. Three years before I had created a monster of superhuman strength. Now I was about to finish another. What would she be like? I was struck with the thought that she might be a thousand times more evil than her mate. What if she delighted in murder and destruction? My monster had sworn to leave the world of man. What if this new creature refused to go? What if they hated each other on sight?

Or worse! I thought with horror. What if they had children? Could they not create a whole new race of monsters who could bring terror, death, and destruction to all of mankind? Had I the right to take this chance? Future ages might curse me as the creator of a new evil. Was I trying to buy my own peace at the risk of the whole human race?

I trembled and my heart sank. I looked up and through the window I saw the monster. His lips were twisted in a ghastly grin. He had followed me! He had come now to see that I fulfilled my promise. His face looked full of evil. I had been mad to promise him another creature like himself!

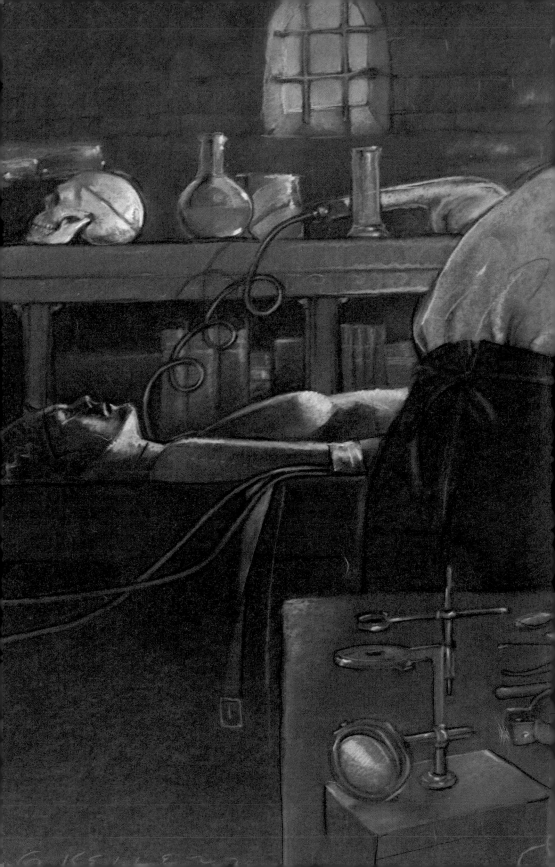

With a cry of rage, I sprang to my feet. Before me was the nearly-completed form of the female monster. Trembling with passion, I tore the evil thing to pieces. Outside, the monster saw me destroy the creature — his hope for happiness. A howl of rage came from those black lips. He left the window and soon I heard his footsteps on the path. The door opened and before me stood the monster.

"You have broken your promise!" he cried. "You have destroyed your work! And you have destroyed all my hopes."

"Yes!" I answered. "Be gone! Never will I create another hideous and wicked creature like yourself!"

The monster gnashed his teeth in rage. "Shall every other man have a mate and I be alone? Are you to be happy while I live in misery? Man, you shall repent of the harm you have done me! Soon you will curse the very light of day!"

"Stop, devil!" I cried. "Leave me. I will never change my mind!"

"Then beware. I am fearless and powerful. I will watch and wait. I will be with you on your wedding night!"

Before I could move, he was gone. All was silent, but his words rang in my ears. I burned with rage to follow him and kill the murderer of my peace of mind. I shuddered to think who might be the next victim of his revenge. I thought again of his words: "I will be with you on your wedding night!" This, then, was the time he had fixed for my death, but I would not die without a struggle.

The next morning I left my island. The sea was rough and my boat was tossed and carried to a distant shore. I had no idea where I was. A village was nearby, and as I pulled the boat onto the sand, several people came towards me.

"My good friends," I called. "Will you be so kind as to tell me the name of this town?"

"You will know soon enough," replied one man.

I was surprised at the rude answer and even more surprised when the men took my arms and pulled me along towards the village. I was alarmed by the anger I saw in their faces.

"Where are we going?" I asked.

"We are taking you to see the judge. You will tell him what you know about a gentleman who was murdered here last night."

This answer startled me, but I had nothing to fear. I had committed no crime. We were soon joined by the judge, and I was taken to a room where the corpse lay. How can I describe what I saw? I can still feel the horror and pain. There in the coffin lay the lifeless form of my beloved friend Henry!

The human mind can only stand so much agony. I was carried from the room in strong convulsions. I had no doubt who had killed Henry. This was the beginning of the monster's revenge. Never was a man so miserable as I.

For two months I lay in a fever near death. At the end of that time I awakened to find my father beside me. I stretched out my hand to him. "You are safe!" I cried. "And Elizabeth and Ernest? Are they safe also?"

My father calmed me and assured me that all was well at home. But my troubles were not over. I looked around the room and found that I was in a prison. I was to be tried for Henry's murder! Thankfully the jury was presented evidence that proved I was on the island on the night of the murder. At last I was free to go home.

Many times during the long nights of our journey I cried out in my sleep. My father asked me what I meant by my wild words. What was this monster? But I could not tell him. He would think I was mad.

As we traveled, my father spoke often about Elizabeth. She was waiting for the day when we could be married. Always when I thought about our marriage, the words of the monster came back to me: "I will be with you on your wedding night!"

This was to be my punishment. On that night he would

kill me and snatch away my hope of happiness. Well, so be it. I would fight. If he won, I would be dead and his power over me would end. If I killed him, however, I would be a free man!

When we arrived in Geneva, Elizabeth welcomed me with love. Tears, however, filled her eyes when she saw my thin body and fevered cheeks. She, too, was much thinner from worry.

Often in the days that followed I burned with rage or sat silent and miserable. Elizabeth alone had the power to soothe me. Her gentle voice calmed me and gave me courage. Sometimes I believed it would be better if I left. Elizabeth loved me — I had no doubt of this. If the monster killed me, what pain would my death bring her! But I could not leave my beloved again. I had to have her. So the date for our wedding was set. We decided that immediately after the marriage we would go to a cottage on the edge of Lake Como. In the meantime I took care to protect myself. I carried a pistol and a dagger with me wherever I went. But I saw no sign of the monster.

The wedding was a joyful occasion. A large party gathered at my father's house afterwards. When Elizabeth and I finally set out for the lake, the sun was low in the heavens. It was eight o'clock when we arrived. The wind had been soft, but now it blew strongly. Clouds swept across the sky, and a heavy rain began to fall.

I had been calm all day, but as night came, I was afraid. Elizabeth saw the fear on my face and her hands began to tremble.

"What is it that frightens you, Victor?" she asked.

"Oh! Peace, my love," I replied. "After tonight, all will be safe. Go to bed now. I am going to sit up awhile."

She left me, and I walked through the house. I looked in every corner where the monster might be hiding. Where was he? Had something prevented him from coming?

Even as the thought crossed my mind, I heard a shrill and dreadful scream. It came from the room where Eliza-

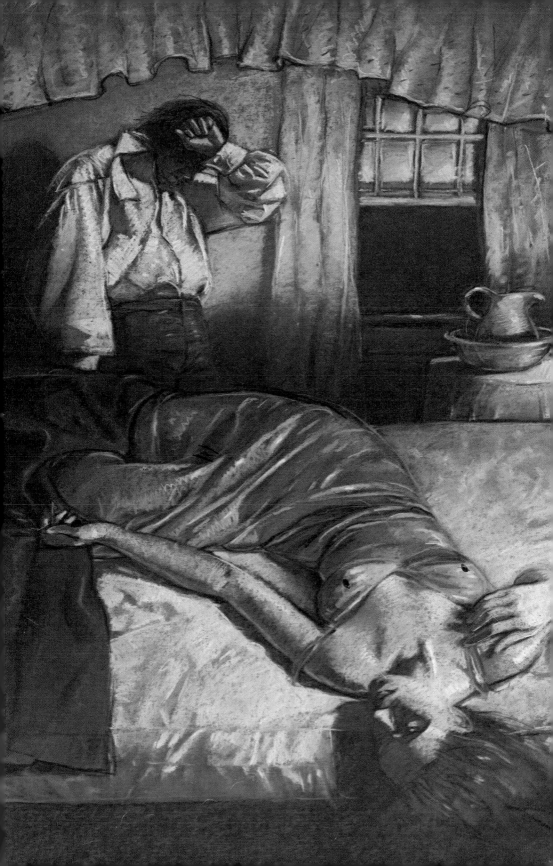

beth slept. The scream was repeated, and I rushed into the bedroom.

Great God! Why did I not die then and there? Across the bed lay Elizabeth — dead. The marks of the monster's fingers were on her neck. Her head hung down and her twisted face was half covered by her hair. I ran to her and held her cold body in my arms.

Suddenly my eyes went to the window. There in the yellow light of the moon I saw the monster — a hideous grin on his face. I rushed forward and took the pistol from my coat. I fired, but he escaped. He ran with the swiftness of lightning and jumped into the lake.

The storm had died with my beloved Elizabeth, and through the stillness of the night, I heard a terrible and evil laugh. As the laughter faded away, I heard the monster's voice: "I am satisfied, my creator. You, too, now live in misery, and I am satisfied!"

That is the end of my tale, Robert. For months now, I have followed the monster. I followed him through all of Europe, across the Black Sea, through Russia, here to the wilderness of the Arctic. Still he escapes me. The day you found me, I saw him not more than a mile ahead, but before I could catch up with him, the ice broke and I was left on the floating ice raft. The monster had escaped me again. And what will happen now? I know I will never leave your ship alive. Must I die and he yet live?

EPILOGUE

Letter to Mrs. Saville from Robert Walton — continued.

My dear sister, you have now read the strange tale of Victor Frankenstein. But there is more to come.

Even as my new friend finished speaking, I knew that he had spoken the truth. His life was nearly over. He fell into an easy sleep where he spoke aloud with his dead loved ones. I knew that he then looked forward to the peace that death would bring. I sat beside his bed. His hand pressed mine, his lips became silent, and his eyes closed forever.

I left him to go up on deck and look around at the sea of ice. My own adventure was nearly over. Soon the cold and ice would force us to return home. The wind froze the tears on my cheeks, and I returned to my cabin. The sight that met my eyes was so horrible, I don't know if I can write of it.

There by the bed of my dead friend stood a monster! He was a giant — huge and ugly. Long locks of ragged hair hid part of his face. Never had I seen such a hideous sight. When he saw me, he sprang towards the window, but I called on him to stay. He paused, looked at me, and then again turned towards the dead body of Victor Frankenstein.

"This is also my victim!" he exclaimed. "In his murder my crimes are finished. Oh, Frankenstein! Noble man! I can no longer ask you to pardon me my sins."

His voice was filled with tears, and I could not help but

pity this hideous monster. "You repent too late," I said. "If you had repented earlier, Frankenstein would still be alive."

"Do you think he hated me more than I hated myself?" the monster cried. "Once I hoped to find people who would forgive my ugly form, but the good in me was killed by the cruelty and prejudice of mankind. I longed for love and friendship, but always I was hated and rejected. Why do you hate me more than those people who made me what I am? Even now my mind burns with rage when I think about the injustice of the world.

"But fear not," he continued, "that I will sin again. My work is now complete. I will leave your ship and build a fire. When the flames grow high, I will burn this hideous body of mine. I shall die, and when the fire fades away, my ashes will be swept into the sea by the winds. My spirit will sleep in peace. He is dead who created me. When I am dead, both of us will be forgotten. Farewell!"

He sprang from the cabin window and onto the ice raft below. He was soon carried away by the waves and lost in darkness and distance.

GLOSSARY

anatomy   (ə nat′ ə me)   the parts of a body and how they go together

charnel house   (charn′ əl   haus)   a place where bodies or bones are kept

convulsion   (kən vəl′ shən)   an uncontrolled fit in which the muscles tighten up and relax

deformed   (dih formd′)   having an abnormal shape

hideous   (hid′ ē əs)   very ugly; shocking to see

laboratory   (lab′ rə tōr ē)   a room or building where experiments and tests in science are done

miserable   (miz′ rə bəl)   being very unhappy or distressed

revenge   (ri venj′)   the act of hurting someone because you think that person has hurt you